The Magic Knight

MARY B. PALMER

Illustrated by Bill Sokol

1 9 6 4

HOUGHTON MIFFLIN COMPANY BOSTON

The Riverside Press Cambridge

To the Muse

1

ONE summer's day a number of hundred years ago, the sun came up precisely as the moon went down. Loquid the Sea Serpent, lying stretched out on the cold sand beside his cave, woke just in time to see what was going on out of the corner of each eye.

"Now *that*," he said to himself, "is a most important omen. Something extraordinary is bound to happen today. Whatever it is and wherever it is, I must be there."

He shook himself wide awake, feeling pleased and expectant. Through all ninety-three feet of him he felt the urge to be off. Mrs. Loquid was still asleep. So he slithered silently into the sea, unnoticed and pretending not to remember that it was Monday morning and he had work to do.

Loquid lived at the northern rim of the flat world. Until this morning he had always kept dutifully to his job of scaring sailors away from the earth's edge. Today he decided they could take care of themselves. He sensed he might have more interesting things to do.

And he was right.

The day, begun so pleasantly with the omen, continued with an unusual encounter. He had been swimming along happily through seas he had never swum before when he suddenly ran THUMP into a small sailboat with a boy at the helm.

"Ouch!" said Loquid, licking the sore spot over his left eyebrow.

"Ouch!" said the boy from the bottom of the boat. The collision had snapped his mast and sent him tumbling into the bilge where he lay in a confusion of ropes and canvas.

"Why don't you look where you're going?" the Sea Serpent complained. "You hurt me."

"You broke my mast!" the boy retorted, struggling to his feet and trying to put the boat to rights.

"Is that bad?"

"Of course it's bad! I can't sail without a mast."

He looked furious as he fussed about trying to tidy things up.

"Everything's been very bad for months and months," he added angrily.

"Has it?" Loquid asked with interest.

The boy didn't answer. Instead, he pulled out

an oar and began sculling his little vessel toward a sandbar. Loquid followed alongside, graciously making no further reference to his sore eyebrow and waiting to see what might come of this chance meeting. It was a bright and balmy day. He enjoyed the swim.

Once arrived at the sandbar, the boy continued to ignore his escort, pulling his boat out of the water and looking around for some way to mend his mast.

"Tell me what's been bad for months and months," Loquid said as he heaved himself up on the sand.

"Can't you see I'm busy," the boy snapped. "I can't talk about it now. And it wouldn't do any good if I *could*."

"Might, you know," the Sea Serpent replied placidly. "Something important is going to happen today. I knew it when I saw the sun come up *precisely* as the moon went down. You notice that?"

"No," said the boy.

"What's going to happen might be bad, but on the other hand it might be good. Personally, I'm

more inclined toward the latter. Whichever way it is, I have a feeling you're part of it."

"If I'm in it, it's bad," the boy said sulkily. "And so far all *you've* done is make things worse. This isn't even my boat!"

"Whose is it?"

"Prince Gillian's."

"And who are you?"

"Quist, his page."

"Now that's better," Loquid said pleasantly. "Now we're having a proper talk. My name's Loquid. How about some lunch?"

"Whose?" Quist asked, noting the Sea Serpent's glance at the basket in the boat.

"Yours, of course. I haven't got any."

"First you bust my mast and then you want my lunch!" the page fumed. "Just because you're bigger than I am, I suppose."

"I'm a good deal bigger but I'm also a good deal calmer. Heavens, the way you fuss you'll never figure anything out. Eating helps thinking, by the way."

Quist looked skeptical, but he opened the basket anyway, producing an ample meal of plovers' eggs, pickles, and cheese. Food did seem to calm him down at that. Soon he found himself telling the Sea Serpent all the bad things that had been happening to him over the last months — even though he couldn't see how his cumbersome new acquaintance could possibly help him.

2

AND so it came about that Quist the Page told Loquid the Sea Serpent all about his life at the court of Ilfinore, starting at the very beginning.

It had all begun on a quite ordinary day, he told his listener. He and his father were working together on the shore, scraping the barnacles off their fishing boat to ready her for sea again. For some time Quist had had an uncomfortable feeling of being watched, and when he finally turned to look, had seen a tall man on a white stallion above him on the cliff. He was shading his eyes and staring straight at him.

As their eyes met, the man shouted to him, beckoning him to come. Quist asked his father who the stranger might be, and when his father had straightened up and had a good look himself, he told him he was Argoth, the King of Ilfinore — though heaven knew what he might want with him. He had best go quickly and find out.

"When I got up on the cliff," Quist told Loquid, "the King said he thought I might be just the boy

he was looking for. He said I seemed a practical type — the sort who would bring back what he was sent for. If I was told to catch a fish, I caught a fish — didn't I? I said I did if there were any to catch, and he said naturally, he understood that. But I wouldn't dawdle about on the beach picking up seashells, would I? And I said no, I wouldn't do that. So he said, 'Come to the castle tomorrow and I'll make you my son's page.' He said I would be good for Prince Gillian."

"Why?" Loquid asked.

Quist said he had no idea himself at the time. He had talked it over with his father who was puzzled, too. His father told him that Prince Gillian was a great disappointment to everyone in the court. He alone of all the young men his age had not yet won his spurs and been knighted. Since he was the King's son, this was particularly embarrassing.

"I don't understand," said Loquid. "What was he supposed to do to get knighted?"

"Something very brave," Quist said.

King Argoth kept setting the Prince a series of Deeds to Do, Quist explained, to prove his worthiness for knighthood. But at each task in turn,

Gillian failed hopelessly — though always cheerfully, returning to the castle with souvenirs and full of the wonders he had seen. When he was sent to recover treasure from under the sea, for instance, he came back instead with an electric eel which he kept in a tank of salt water in his room for reading by at night. When he was sent to slay a Griffin, he couldn't even find him, though he returned with a marvelous drawing of what he thought he looked like. In fact, the Prince's main interest and greatest talent was art. He could paint fine landscapes and seascapes and portraits. But none of these things impressed the King.

"My father said maybe the King thought I could help the Prince in some way, though he didn't see how. Anyway, it was all right for me to go. So I went."

Quist had never been in the castle before. It was up the hill from the town, protected by a massive wall and topped by a multitude of turrets. Inside the portico and surrounding the courtyard were dozens of dark little rooms — a cabbage room, wheat bins, an armory, and workshops for tinsmiths, blacksmiths, shoemakers, falconers and carpenters — and a maze of tunnels and passages that Quist longed to explore.

But on that first day, he was taken directly to the Great Hall to get his instructions from the King. He was told to kneel on the bearskin rug at the foot of the throne and speak only when spoken to.

Presently Argoth entered. Quist was awed by the sheer bulk of him, dressed in his official robes of velvet and ermine with his jeweled crown like the glittering peak of a mountain rising far above. From where Quist knelt, all he could see of the King's face was his great black beard and cavernous nostrils. The royal voice boomed through the royal beard, ordering him in a most solemn manner to be faithful to the court and to keep the Prince's mind on what he was supposed to do.

"We appoint thee Royal Page," the King intoned. Then he sat down on his throne and Queen Argotha slithered in beside him. Quist didn't know that this was a signal for him to get up and go, so he stayed where he was.

Suddenly bugles blew and knights appeared and ladies in cone-shaped hats emerged on balconies and the whole thing was very bewildering. Quist squirmed around to see what was going on. He was about to be removed bodily by a guard when the Queen leapt from her seat, swooped down on him like a swallow, and gently wafted him to one side.

She got him out of the way just in time before the big oaken doors of the hall swung open to admit the portly presences of Lords Battledore and Shuttlecock, a pair of visiting dignitaries. For a minute, Quist had imagined all the pageantry was for him: he blushed when he realized it wasn't. He blushed even more when the Queen patted him on the head and said, "There, there," as though he were a mere child. In that uncomfortable moment he decided he was going to be the strongest and bravest page in all the court of Ilfinore, by Appointment to His Majesty, King Argoth I. He threw back his shoulders in imitation of the knights around him and tried looking neutral the way they did, as though he saw such sights daily.

He managed pretty well through the Parade and the Presentation of Flags, but when Lord Battledore's wig slipped off and Lord Shuttlecock absentmindedly picked it up and put it on his own head, he had to bite his tongue to keep a straight face.

"Good chap," came a whisper in his ear.

It was Prince Gillian. He had arrived late, as usual, and was not dressed properly, as usual, and was whispering when he shouldn't be, as usual. Quist decided the best thing to do was to scowl. So he did.

Prince Gillian scowled back at him. And so the two of them stood frowning through the rest of the ceremony. This caused favorable comment afterwards and made people say that the new page was going to be good for Gillian. Now he might straighten up, win his spurs, and become a proper knight. For actually most of the people in the court were more interested in Gillian's future than they were in Lords Battledore and Shuttlecock. Visiting dignitaries happened every Thursday on Visiting Dignitaries Day — coming and going in a rather meaningless way with creamed chicken for lunch. Gillian belonged to Ilfinore and meant more to them.

"Let's go," the Prince whispered a few minutes later.

Quist pretended not to hear. He had a feeling they were supposed to stay to the end, and anyway he was enjoying himself.

"Come on," Gillian said.

Quist didn't budge.

A dancing bear was led onto the floor by the court jester. The bear wore a foolish hat with a flower in it. He went around and around to the beat of a drum and the jangling of tambourines.

"I like outdoor bears better," Gillian said impatiently. "Come on now — it's an order!"

3

RELUCTANTLY, Quist followed his new master up
to his room in the west tower. There they found
Urga, the lumbering old housekeeper, standing
in the middle of the room bellowing orders to a
host of younger maids who swarmed over everything like so many beetles. There was a final flurry
of feather dusters as the Prince came in before they
scampered away, giggling.

Behind them, they left an awesome cleanliness.
Everything that could be put away was carefully
hidden from sight; everything that couldn't was
lined up in rows. Stone floor, rafters, walls, the
big worktable — even the Prince's paint pots —
had all been scrubbed and polished until they shone
like mirrors. The bed was made with the quilt
tucked in so tight it looked as hard as wood. The
picture Gillian had been painting that morning
was nowhere to be seen. His easel had been folded
and put in a corner.

"It's unlivable," Gillian sighed.

"Poof!" said Urga, and turned on her heel. She

and Gillian had been having this battle since he was a mere princeling. Urga always won.

"Well, I might as well get on with it," Gillian said, sitting gingerly on the edge of his immaculate bed. "I wanted to paint this afternoon, but I can't now."

"What do you have to do?" Quist asked.

"Joust with Grugeon."

"Do what with who, sir?"

Gillian didn't answer. He was looking sadly around his room, shaking his head.

"Everybody isn't like everybody else," he said finally, sounding as though he was talking to himself. "Not even all princes are alike. Or am I the only prince in the world who likes to paint?"

Quist felt uncomfortable. He didn't know what to say. He was wondering what sort of job he had got himself into.

"Do you realize," Gillian went on, "that you just can't go on with a painting if someone cleans up all the colors you've mixed specially, and washes off your palette?"

"I suppose you can't," Quist said. "But don't you care about being knighted?"

18

"Not much. A little, I suppose. I mean if I get knighted they'll leave me alone and I won't have to joust or do Deeds if I don't want to."

He got up and went over to a brass-bound chest and opened it. He handed Quist a quantity of padded clothing, explaining it was meant to keep him from getting hurt when he was jousting. He had the new page help him dress.

"I've been trying to think what to do with you," Gillian said. "I've never had a page before. I guess you're meant to carry things. Other pages do. My father's page carries his crown, for instance. The knights' pages carry their helmets. There must be a reason — not that knights can't carry things exactly, but . . ."

"But what?"

"I don't know. Maybe so they'll have their hands free to do other things. Fight perhaps? Bow to ladies? It's clumsy with an armful of bundles. Awkward to drop a helmet on a lady's toe. *You* know."

He handed Quist his helmet to carry. On their way down to the jousting yard they had no fights and met no ladies. Quist was disappointed. He wanted to see what Gillian would do.

Grugeon was waiting in the yard, pacing up and down and grumbling. He was an ugly fellow with matted hair and biceps as big as melons. He stood two heads over Gillian — and Gillian was a good height himself. His greeting to the Prince was barely civil. To Quist he said nothing at all until Gillian had mounted his horse. Then it was only to yell at him to give the Prince his helmet and hop to it.

When Grugeon, too, was mounted, swinging his thick right leg over the saddle and thrusting his spurred boots into the stirrups, he rode his horse straight at Quist — quite purposefully — making the page leap for the safety of the wall.

"That'll teach you to keep out of the way," he shouted, giving Quist a savage look as he wheeled away.

Gillian hadn't noticed. He was fiddling with his helmet. It didn't seem to fit right and looked uncomfortable. He was having trouble adjusting the visor with his left hand while his right grasped the heavy lance to hold it straight in its socket.

"Are you ready, sir?" Grugeon called. His question sounded more like an order. His horse pawed the ground and snorted, seeming as anxious as its master to get on with it.

"Oh I guess so," Gillian answered. He gave a final snap to his helmet, grabbed the lance in both hands, spurred his horse and bore down on Grugeon in fine style. But all his teacher had to do was to sidestep his horse a foot or two and the Prince's lance hit not him, but the wall. Gillian was hurled into the air like a pole vaulter — coming to rest astride the wall right next to his page.

"Ooof!" he said, leaning forward and rubbing his bottom. "Say, Grugeon, do you think I could do that again? Would they give me anything for acrobatics? A couple of points maybe toward my spurs?"

He sounded cheerful. But his teacher, like his father, was not pleased. Grugeon had no sense of humor. He only swore under his breath and waited for the Prince to get back down.

And so it went for most of the afternoon, although Gillian never again landed so neatly on the

wall. He landed every place else; on the ground, in the rosebushes, sometimes on his hands as though he were doing a cartwheel. He went through his paces good-naturedly, mounting and dismounting, trotting, cantering, charging — and inevitably ending by falling, albeit gracefully. When he picked himself up, he would smile broadly and suggest they try it again. He never got ruffled. He never apologized. He seemed to listen attentively to his instructor, cocking his head to one side and even asking intelligent questions.

But he never got it right.

Through all the Prince's good cheer, Grugeon got sourer and sourer. In the end it was the teacher and not the pupil who lost patience and called a halt. He looked more worn out than Gillian, though he hadn't been unseated once himself.

"I'll take my things back," Gillian called up to Quist. "You help Grugeon."

Quist didn't like that idea at all but he had no choice. He dropped down from the wall, watching his new master walk jauntily away with his helmet under his arm.

"I hope he meets a lady and drops it on her foot!" he muttered to himself.

"What's that?" Grugeon asked, looking up from loosening the girth on his horse.

"I said it's a nice day," Quist answered quickly. He wanted no trouble with this fellow.

"Nice DAY!"

He straightened his aching shoulders and spat a great spit.

"You think it's a nice day with a fool of a prince like that? You think I like to train such an idiot? *You'll* be sorry you're his page. Wait and see. You can't do no more for him than the rest of us!"

He yanked the saddle from his horse and flung it vengefully on the ground.

"Now take that thing to the stable," he commanded.

Quist did as he was told, and in silence. When he came back, Grugeon had the Prince's horse unsaddled and together they led the two mounts to the stable, washed and curried them and gave them their oats. Grugeon never stopped muttering the whole time.

"Dumbest, stupidest prince I ever saw!"

"Have you seen many?" Quist finally asked.

"No, I haven't. None others at all. And thank heaven for that! But I've known and taught gentry enough, I have — dukes and earls and counts and marquises. I've trained the whole bag of them to be first-rate jousters. The Duke of Ollyp won the National Festive last year, hands down — and *he* was one of my boys."

The memory seemed to mellow him a bit. He invited Quist to come along with him to the kitchen for supper.

The kitchen was in the cellar of the castle. It was a huge room broken up into compartments by thick stone arches that supported the beams and floor of the Great Hall above. In the daytime it was a dim place, lit only by tiny grated windows near the ceiling. Now, at twilight, the torches were burning, giving the room a more cheerful aspect. Supper had started as the two came in.

Urga presided over the head table, grand as a queen, while the scullery maids hovered about her offering tasty morsels. She scolded Grugeon for being late, and sent him out again to wash. To

Quist's surprise, Grugeon obeyed her meekly. He asked the other pages at his table how this could be, and they told him Grugeon was in love with Urga. He would do anything she told him to do. He was always hanging about the kitchen trying to catch her eye, but she paid no attention to him unless she wanted the use of his muscles for some heavy work. Once he even wrote her a love poem, leaving it under her soup bowl. But if she read it or liked it, she never let on to him.

Quist also learned that night how people made fun of Prince Gillian for never doing anything right. The other pages boasted of all the things their masters could do, how brave they were, and how nice they looked in their armor. And they showed off their own knowledge of boar hunts and heraldry and how to carry crowns on cushions.

Quist had nothing to say. He was glad when supper was over and he could get away.

"I should think you would have been," Loquid said as he heard this part of the story. "Didn't things get any better?"

"For a while they did," Quist answered. "It wasn't like that all the time."

4

AFTER a rather bad start, Quist went on, the next weeks were happy ones. He explored every inch of the castle from dungeons to parapets. He made friends with the grooms and learned to ride. He spent long hours with Thrag, the blacksmith, helping him shoe the knights' horses, and listening to stories of glorious battles. He got used to Grugeon, more or less, and kept out of his way as much as he could.

King Argoth was a great believer in Physical Fitness, he discovered, so that every morning he made the knights do push-ups in the castle courtyard before breakfast. Quist never missed the scene. The King and Queen were always there, standing on a balcony to watch — Argoth urging on the knights and Argotha making small admiring squealing noises. Then everyone would go inside for hot scones and mugs of scalding tea.

Prince Gillian was never present; neither pushing up nor looking down. He took no interest in things his father cared about and much in things

the King thought unimportant. He used the exercise time to work on a design for a mural he wanted to paint in the Great Hall someday.

Quist didn't have much work because the Prince couldn't think what to do with him. He slept in the tower room and helped Gillian find his clothes in the morning, and reminded him of appointments he had, and carried his helmet for him for the jousting lessons. Often they went sailing together in Gillian's skiff, but that was pure pleasure. There was nothing the page liked better. He dreamed of someday having a boat of his own.

Then came the morning when Gillian and Quist were summoned to the King's private quarters to be told of the Prince's next Deed.

Word had reached Argoth that there was a damsel in distress on the mountain, kept prisoner by the Goroblast. Gillian was to set out at once to rescue the maiden and bring back the beast, dead or alive. If he should succeed — for once — in this dangerous mission, he would be promptly knighted and everyone would be much relieved.

"Now get on with it!" King Argoth finished, dismissing them both from his Royal Presence and turning back to his plans for the next tournament. It was clear that the King was happier with this task than with sending his son on missions: tournaments would take place just as he scheduled them. He was never sure about his son.

"What's the Goroblast?" Quist asked as soon as he and Gillian had got back to the Prince's room.

"I don't know exactly," Gillian said. "Urga used to talk about him. You know — if you don't wash behind your ears or eat your oatmeal, the Goroblast will get you. Things like that. I don't know what he looks like. Did she say once that he had nine heads? Or was that another beast?"

"I wouldn't want to try to kill a beast with nine heads," Quist said, shuddering. "If you chopped off one, he'd come right back at you with another."

"That's not what bothers me so much," Gillian said. "It's all that *thinking*. If he has nine heads to think with he must be a genius."

"Maybe that's how he knows when people don't eat their oatmeal — being a genius."

They continued to discuss the matter as they packed. Gillian finally decided it wasn't the Goroblast that was nine-headed. He had him confused

31

with another horrid beast who bit little boys who told lies. What the Goroblast looked like Urga had never said.

Quist suggested they had better take oatmeal and facecloths along in any case so that they wouldn't offend the beast needlessly or have him bursting in on their camp before they were ready to deal with him.

So they packed these things along with a change of clothes, and armed themselves, and went down to the stable for the horses. There Gillian left Quist to fill the saddlebags with their gear while he said a quick goodbye to his mother.

When they were jogging along the road together outside the castle walls, Gillian told Quist that his mother had cried at his going, as she always did, and had given him an apple tart to put in his pocket. Queen Argotha had baked it herself that morning. But since she had never cooked anything before in her life, it had turned out badly. Quist thought to himself of his own mother's good cooking, but he said nothing. He just let his slice drop in a blackberry bush when the Prince wasn't looking. Gillian himself didn't seem to notice. He ate his piece absentmindedly, the way he attended to all practical matters.

It was Quist who had to keep both their minds on what they were doing. Whereas Gillian was forever wanting to trot off to look at a beautiful view or follow a fox's tracks, Quist kept them on the trail that led to the mountain. He found himself constantly calling to the Prince to get him back — as though he were the older instead of the younger of the two.

After a while they came to a darksome wood, padded soft with pine needles so that the horses' hooves made no sound. It was a silent place, and Gillian and Quist were silent too. Even the smells were still in this windlessness so that they rode from an invisible layer of scent of balsam into another of pine and beyond into spruce. Both horses and riders twitched their nostrils to take in all the good smells.

In the middle of the forest they came on a girl in a nightgown sitting in an oak. She had long, straight red hair, and in her lap was a lyre.

"Look," Quist whispered, drawing up close to Gillian. "Do you think she's the damsel in distress?"

"Maybe," Gillian whispered back. "But I don't see the Goroblast anywhere."

"He might be hiding," Quist said, patting the hilt of his dagger and looking around suspiciously. But he could see nothing ominous in the shadows.

Gillian rode ahead. He was almost at the foot of the tree before the girl saw him. She let out a small "Ooops!" and scrambled up higher until she was entirely hidden by leaves.

"Wait!" Gillian called up to her. "Let me talk to you!"

A small pink nose poked out between the leaves, withdrew, and reappeared. Two green eyes stared down at prince and page.

"We won't hurt you," Gillian went on in his gentlest tone. "We just want to know if you're the damsel in distress."

"Which damsel? What *sort* of distress?" the girl asked without venturing from her hiding place.

"Are you the one the Goroblast is keeping prisoner?"

"Oh don't be silly! Of course not!"

No longer timid, the girl slid back down into the crotch of the tree where she had first been sitting.

"He couldn't keep me prisoner even if he wanted to," she said snippily. "I can *fly*."

She twisted around so that Gillian could see her wings. He told her they were very pretty. Quist wanted to see her fly, but she said she never did unless she was going somewhere.

"And right now I've nowhere to go. That's *my* distress."

She put her head on one side and began to look Gillian over.

"What's more, I think that's partly *your* fault," she went on, frowning.

"How could it be?" Gillian asked in surprise.

"Because I'm a Muse, and my guess is you're an artist. It's my job to inspire people like you — painters and musicians and poets — to fly about and play to you on my lyre. How can I do that if you're not even *trying* to create anything?"

"I'm sorry," the Prince said. "I have to do a Deed today."

"Hmmmmmmmph!" said the Muse, striking a nasty discord on her lyre that made her visitors flinch. "THAT for you — and all the rest of the lazy people who make excuses! Do you know that right this minute there isn't one single person in all of Ilfinore who's trying to create anything?"

Gillian said he didn't know that. For himself, he'd much rather be back in his tower room, painting. He hoped she would come visit him next time he was working because he could certainly use some help.

But the Muse wouldn't listen to him. She yawned and swung her bare legs and turned up her toes. And just when he was in the middle of telling her about the mural he was planning, she suddenly sat up straight and told him to shush.

"Someone *is* trying!" she exclaimed. "I can hear him."

"I can't hear anything," Quist said, straining his ears.

"That's because you're not a Muse. It's a sound inside your head."

"How do you . . ." Quist began.

"Shhh! How can I hear over your buzzing?" she snapped at him. "Let me think what the thinker is thinking."

She pushed her hair back and wiggled her ears.

"Is it," the Muse mused, "a split infinitive or a hanging participle? A painting that needs a daub of red in the right-hand corner? An A-flat where a sharp should be?"

Elated now, she stood up in the tree crotch, legs astride and hands on her hips.

"Oh! Now I know what it is! It's a poet! And he's stuck on a rhyme for . . . for . . . for *octopus!*" she cried triumphantly.

"Yoo-hoo!" she called. "Wait for me. I'm coming!"

And therewith she tucked her lyre under one arm, pressed her fingers together like a diver, gave a hop, and flew off, barely grazing the top of Gillian's head. He ducked automatically, but the Muse was a skillful flyer who had never had an accident yet. Within seconds she gained altitude.

Quist and Gillian heard her crying "Octopus,

boctopus, coctopus, doctopus," as she disappeared from view over the tree tops.

"What a marvelous flyer she is!" Gillian said admiringly. "I'd like to know her better."

"But she's only a girl," Quist said. He had little use for girls no matter what they could do. His major interest in this expedition was to catch the Goroblast. Helping Gillian win his spurs came second. Saving a damsel was a poor third. Having anything to *do* with the damsel didn't figure at all. It might be nice if she admired you, of course, and told you how brave you were. But no more than that.

These were his thoughts as he waited impatiently for the Prince to start up the trail again. But Gillian didn't move.

"I think I'll paint," he announced. He swung down from his horse and began to unbuckle his saddle bag.

"Oh no!" Quist groaned. "You can't do that. We've got a Deed to do."

The Prince extracted a paintbrush and thoughtfully ran its sable tip down his long nose.

"Can't paint?" he asked, looking plaintively at Quist.

"Can't paint."

"Oh blast. How did I get stuck with *you?* Don't you see that if I started painting, the Muse might come back? She'll never find a rhyme for octopus anyway."

This is a fine turnabout, thought Quist: a page telling his master what to do. But King Argoth had picked him because he was practical and told him to keep Gillian's mind on the job at hand.

"How about a little bird-watching, then?" Gillian said in his most beguiling tone.

"No. No painting. No bird-watching. Please, sir . . ."

Gillian laughed and sprang back into his saddle.

"Call me Gill," he said. "You're doing your job and you're doing it just fine. Now see if you can keep up with me!"

With that the Prince put spurs to his horse and cantered off along the forest trail as skillfully as he sailed a boat. To his surprise, Quist had all he could do to keep him in sight. He didn't seem at all like the bungler he'd watched in the jousting yard. Quist spurred his own horse and rode joyously along the trail. When he burst out of the forest onto the moors, he glimpsed Gillian galloping away into the distance, his cape streaming out behind. He only caught up with him when the Prince was forced to slow his horse for an uphill climb.

They both laughed as they reined their horses.

"Bring on the Goroblast!" Gillian shouted, unsheathing his sword and waving it in the air.

"Bring him on!" shouted Quist. He felt very brave and dashing sitting astride his steed on the mountain path in the late afternoon sun.

"Bless my stars! Two nice young gentlemen!" someone said in a high squeaky voice. "Oh, thank goodness you're here!"

And out of the bushes came a spindly grayhaired woman, dog-trotting up to them and chattering the whole way.

"Come to help a damsel in distress, haven't you, dears? Come from the good King himself, may his name be blessed. Ooo, hoo, what a time I've had. What a shocking time!"

She shook her head violently to emphasize the

41

point, strewing the path with a multitude of hair-pins as she did so.

Gillian jumped down from his horse to help her pick them up.

"It's no matter if we don't find them all," she said as she searched about in the grass. "I can whittle myself a new set in no time at all. Just slivers of whalebone, that's all they are. We've more important business than *this* to worry about, haven't we, sir?"

She straightened up and winked at Gillian, but gave him no time to reply.

"Come straight from the King to help a spinster-damsel, you and your strapping bodyguard here. Oh, the two of you should take care of that mon-ster for sure, you should. You'll be the end of him, I can see that. Your shouts just now made an echo in my heart."

"We'll do our best, ma'am," the Prince said modestly.

"Just tell us where to find him," Quist chimed in.

"There's no such rush as all that," the spinster-damsel said. "It's coming on dark now and no moon tonight. You're better off on a full stomach and a night's sleep. There'll be plenty of time to slay the Goroblast tomorrow."

Quist felt let down when Gillian agreed to wait until morning and accepted the spinster-damsel's hospitality. He had been all set to do battle. Yet when their hostess went on about supper, his mouth began to water and he realized he was hungry.

But elderly ladies and boys do not eat the same thing and Quist was destined to remain hungry that night. After he had watered the horses and set them to graze, he came into the spinster-damsel's hut to find Gillian staring glumly at his plate. All that was on it was a lettuce leaf and a carrot. A mug of barley water completed the meal.

"Eat hearty, mates!" the spinster-damsel urged as she nibbled away at her lettuce. "Oh now, what a time I've had! No peace for a minute, with that Goroblast chasing and hounding me, day and night. He's got me cooped up here like a jailbird, he has. I can't get to the village to visit my sister. I can hardly sneak to the spring and back without his following and taunting me. I've

barricaded my door and strung deerhide over the windows, but I know he snoops around outside at night. Not that I'm not armed myself. Oh no, I've taken care of *that*."

As indeed she had. Her furnishings were scanty: her armament enormous. There was only a straw pallet, bench, table and cookpot in the way of ordinary household equipment besides the pewter plates they were eating from. Otherwise the room was nearly choked with lethal weapons. Over the mantel hung a great curved scimitar as big as the spinster-damsel herself. Twenty fishermen's harpoons were strung from the rafters. The walls were lined with bows and arrows, rusty spears, halberds, and slingshots with a pile of stones handy under each one. By the bed lay a monstrous spiked club.

"You two can sleep in the barn," the spinster-damsel said. "You'll have Solly the cow for company and plenty of fresh straw."

Quist was relieved at this news. There certainly wasn't any room to lie down in the hut. As it was, he kept tripping over weapons whenever he tried to move around.

As early as they politely could, prince and page bade their hostess goodnight and retired to their quarters. Even so, with the best will in the world, they had to interrupt her in mid-paragraph. Quite possibly if they had let her, she would have talked all night.

Solly proved as sociable as her mistress. Fortunately, she didn't know how to talk, being only a common cow, but all night long she kept nuzzling up to her visitors, giving them affectionate laps on the forehead with her pink tongue. Although they had a restless night, they forgave her, for next morning the spinster-damsel milked her and they had plenty of fresh milk for their oatmeal.

They made plans with their hostess as they ate their breakfast under an apple tree. The spinster-damsel was to go ahead of them to the spring, carrying her bucket as on any ordinary day. They would follow behind but keep out of sight until the Goroblast appeared to heckle her. They would try to take him alive and brought ropes for this purpose; but they would slay him if he proved too fierce. The spinster-damsel favored slaughter. Gillian was against it.

"Bloodthirsty mite, isn't she?" he whispered to Quist.

Not long after sunrise they were ready. The spinster-damsel set off up the steep mountain path, swinging her bucket happily and singing a song off-key. Quist and Gillian kept to the bushes, leading their horses by their bridles and walking on their toes. The early birds were chirping in the sunshine and yellow and blue mountain flowers waved in the breeze. It seemed impossible to imagine battle on such a day, but the warriors were committed. Their weapons were in their hands.

The spinster-damsel reached the spring with no more interference than an occasional gnat. Quist and Gillian tethered their horses and crouched in the undergrowth waiting tensely for the Goroblast while she filled her pail in the clear water under a mossy bank. But no matter how hard they stared or how closely they listened, they saw and heard nothing out of the ordinary.

Obviously put out, the spinster-damsel began to sing louder and louder. She spilled the water out of her bucket and began beating on it like a drum. She did a highland jig. She plucked blades of grass and blew through them, producing horrid squealing noises that pierced the morning air and sent the birds flying for cover.

But all to no avail. No beast appeared. The spinster-damsel wore herself out and sat down in a slump. Quist and Gillian, their legs aching from crouching and their ears splitting from the racket, came out of their hiding place to talk things over. Since their ambush had failed, it was decided that they would go on to the Goroblast's cave while the distressed damsel would return to her cottage. Luckily she was just exhausted enough to agree. Prince and page breathed a sigh of relief when she jogged away home.

The Goroblast's cave was only a short way from the spring, set 'round with aspen and silver birch which almost hid the opening — itself a narrow slit beyond which nothing but darkness could be seen. Quist and Gillian separated, taking up their posts on either side of the entrance. Presently they heard a stirring within.

"Phew!" said the Goroblast, sticking his long furry head out of the opening. But the instant he saw Gillian's sword, he ducked back in.

"That's a pretty unfriendly way to act," he growled from inside his shelter.

"Come out and fight!" Quist shouted. He felt quite confident now that he saw the beast did, indeed, have only one head.

"Come out and be captured!" Gillian called.

There was no response. The attackers waited a long time quite uselessly. At last they decided to lay siege and smoke him out. They gathered a pile of dry moss and sticks and set them on fire at the cave's entrance. Gillian stood back a way with his sword drawn. Quist climbed up on the ledge overhead, holding a lasso. The fire burned down rapidly becoming a smoke smudge which blew disagreeably into the cave.

The trick worked. After much coughing and sneezing within, the Goroblast came charging out in a huff, heedlessly slipping his head into Quist's noose.

"We've got him!" Quist shouted exultantly. But a second later he was yanked off his perch and dragged halfway to the spring. Gillian sheathed his sword and rushed up to help, grabbing the rope and holding on as hard as he could. The

Goroblast growled, snorted and yanked — but the harder he pulled now the tighter the knot became. Finally he gave up and sat down on his haunches, glaring at them.

"Well, you're a couple of nasty types, I must say," he growled, after a final sneeze. "Did you want to see me about something?"

"We certainly *do*," Gillian said. "What do you think you're doing keeping the spinster-damsel captive?"

"Keeping her from visiting her sister," Quist chimed in.

"Prowling about her hut at night and scaring her away from her spring."

"From *whose* spring?" the Goroblast asked sharply. "This is *my* spring. She's got a perfectly good well of her own in her backyard. But where does she have to come for water? Up here! And what does she have to do when she comes, may I ask? Howl and scream and beat on her bucket!"

"Well . . ." Gillian began.

"It's not her well at all, you know," the Goroblast continued. "It's a very bad situation. This kind of thing leads to reprisals."

"Then you admit to heckling and tormenting her?" Gillian prodded.

"I admit to her *being* heckled and tormented," the Goroblast said mysteriously. He scratched behind an ear with a hind leg and smiled unpleasantly.

"And you go after children who won't eat their oatmeal," Quist added.

"Children who don't eat their oatmeal are *told* I will go after them," the Goroblast corrected. "Not only that: they are informed that I will eat them alive."

"*Do* you?" Quist asked, giving a tug on the rope around the beast's neck.

"Actually I don't care for children," the Goroblast answered haughtily. "I rather fancy oatmeal — which is probably how the story got started. Also how I come to be associated with nightmares. Children who refuse to eat such a delicacy *deserve* to dream about me."

The Goroblast gave his captors a smug look.

"We ought to kill you right here on the spot," Quist said. "Scaring old ladies and small children!"

"You may try if you wish," the Goroblast responded, "but it's exceptionally difficult to kill an ugly rumor."

"Then we'll take you back alive," said Gillian.

"I agree that a live rumor is better than a dead one," said the Goroblast. "More fun for everyone. More to gossip about. I doubt you'll get me back, but there's no harm in your trying. I'm fed up with my reputation anyway."

He yawned and stood up.

"Shall we go?" he asked.

"No tricks now!" Quist said, fingering the hilt of his dagger.

"Poof!" the Goroblast sneered.

He followed nonchalantly at the end of the slack rope as his captors walked back to their horses. For extra precaution they attached a second rope around his neck so that they both had hold of him. Then they jumped in their saddles and started down the mountain path.

As they rode within earshot of the spinster-damsel's hut, the Goroblast let out a great snorting noise which brought the lady to her door waving a cutlass. When she saw the beast roped to the riders' saddles, she gave out a little shriek, dropped her weapon, and dashed off in the direction of the village.

"She'll go tell her sister now," the Goroblast commented. "Maybe she'll even stay there. She certainly can't live up here without me."

Whatever her future plans, it was soon clear that the spinster-damsel had spread word ahead of the Goroblast's capture. As Quist and Gillian came down out of the forest they could see a great crowd of people swarming outside the castle wall waiting for their first glimpse of the captive.

The Goroblast became increasingly ill-tempered. He growled and pulled at the ropes. But Gillian and Quist held tight.

"You'll get knighted *this* time," Quist said triumphantly. "We've done it, Gill, for sure!"

Gillian said he didn't want to count on anything yet. But he admitted it seemed possible. He said he thought the Goroblast could be tamed in time and might make rather a nice pet even though he *was* ugly. Quist couldn't see it.

The two were discussing these matters and much absorbed in them when they reached the outskirts of the crowd. Suddenly realizing the importance of the occasion, they both straightened up and waved grandly.

But instead of the cheers they expected, the crowd burst out laughing. Some jeered as well — among them Grugeon. After one look, he turned on his heel and marched off. Others followed.

Alarmed, Quist and Gillian looked back to see what the Goroblast might be doing.

He was not there. Only two empty nooses dragged behind in the dust.

"I *said* you couldn't squash an ugly rumor," a voice boomed in Gillian's ear. "I'm just a figment of imagination and I'll go right on figmenting!"

Gillian pulled back to see where the Goroblast might be, but there was nothing to be seen. The voice trailed off into nowhere. He had vanished.

Quist rode up alongside the Prince.

"Did you hear something?" he asked anxiously.

"Yes," said Gillian, "but no one will believe it. It's just the way it always is."

And on that dour note they rode silently into the castle courtyard. No one came to greet them except the stableboys who took their horses away.

They retired to Gillian's tower room and their own gloomy thoughts.

King Argoth avoided his son and did not send for him, but Queen Argotha came up in the evening, bringing them a tray of cold pheasant left from dinner.

"*I* never taught you about the Goroblast," she said to Gillian. "I never believed in him. If anyone around here did it must have been Urga."

"Yes it was," the Prince replied. "She was always full of gruesome stories."

"I wish she'd marry Grugeon so they could be gruesome together," said Quist.

That idea cheered them all. The Queen bade them both goodnight in much better spirits.

5

FOR a while after the Goroblast affair, Gillian was left alone. His father scarcely spoke to him. The knights and ladies spoke only behind his back. Grugeon made excuses for canceling jousting classes. Urga and her squadron of underlings cleaned the Prince's room even more viciously than before. Gillian stayed out of their way, making pleasant sallies into the woods with his paints and returning only after the troops had left. He seemed not to notice the whisperings around him but only to be absorbed in his art. He was still working on designs for a mural for the Great Hall, depicting the history of Ilfinore, even though there was little chance his father would agree to the project.

The Prince's days were also lightened by frequent visits from the Muse, for he had learned how to summon her. Just as he had suspected, she had never found a rhyme for "octopus."

Quist took it harder. He wasn't used to failing or being made fun of. Even if people couldn't understand about the Goroblast — and he wasn't sure he quite understood it all himself — he wished at least that they would realize that Gillian was a fine artist who worked just as hard at painting as others did at knocking each other off their horses. He got a good many black eyes and bruises in fist fights with the other pages trying to prove his point. But it remained unproven.

Thrag was the only one who was sympathetic, being a bit of an artist himself who turned out quite tasteful weathervanes and portcullises. But he didn't know how to help. People put up with his kind of art, he told Quist, because it was practical.

"Maybe Gill ought to be a blacksmith, then," Quist suggested.

"No," said Thrag. "He can't be. He was born a prince, poor lad. He's just got to behave like one. He's got to do something gory or splashy before they'll leave him alone to do as he likes."

"What could he do?" Quist asked.

Thrag didn't know. He and the page put a lot of thought into it as they worked together in the smithy. They talked it over this way and that and upside down, but got nowhere.

King Argoth, too, was thinking — which, for a nonthinking type is the hardest work in the world. The tournament he had planned was over and it was off-season for boars so he had some time on his hands. He began spending too much of it alone in his private quarters. In public, he looked gloomy. Queen Argotha became quite worried about him and tried to find ways to unknit his brows. She tried to interest him in a voyage in the royal barge, but he wouldn't go. She brought him cups of raspberry tea. She sang quavery little songs to him at night. At last, quite desperate, she called on Moondroth the Magician to come to the castle and cheer the King with a magic show.

Despite himself, the King enjoyed it. He marveled when Moondroth poured wine out of an empty pitcher, sent plates flying mysteriously about the room and plucked a pair of turtle doves from the Queen's hair. Best of all, he did a sun dance and sent off rockets so that the next day it stopped raining for the first time in a week and the farmers could go back to their planting.

The show and the general acclaim accorded to Moondroth gave the King the idea he had been looking for. He had a long talk with the magician, and then he summoned Gillian to the Royal Presence.

Magic, he explained to his son, was as much admired in Ilfinore as feats of daring. Gillian, having failed at every Deed so far, was now to be given one last change to redeem himself. He was to be apprenticed to Moondroth. When he learned all that Moondroth knew, he was to do something very magical. If he succeeded, he would be knighted forthwith. If he failed, he would be exiled once and for all from the kingdom, and Quist would be sent packing after him.

"I can make a Muse appear," Gillian said.

"Oh, those silly girls!" the King replied impatiently. "Who wants *them* around anyway? No, no. What I want is *useful* magic in the service of the Kingdom. Now get on with it!"

Gillian bowed and left. He knew it was useless to argue.

He went looking for Quist, finally finding him in the smithy.

"Come on," he said gloomily. "This is our last chance. We've got to go to magic school."

Quist followed, though he hadn't the least idea what Gillian was talking about.

Moondroth lived a mile away on the cliff above the town. On the way, the Prince told him what his father had said.

"It ought to be pretty good fun," said Quist.

"It doesn't sound like fun to me," Gillian answered.

Moondroth wasn't pleased either. Nothing short of a Royal Command would have induced him to tell his secrets and teach his trade. Even as it was, King Argoth had had to butter him up by appointing him Professor to the Court of Ilfinore and presenting him with a magnificent scroll illuminated in red and gold, brimming with complimentary phrases and bearing the Royal Crest of crossed dolphins on a sea of marshmallows.

A more grudging professor never lived. Shrouded in his cowled cape, he doled out secrets like a miser his pennies. He tried to make everything take twice as long as necessary, dividing a year's program into such courses as "Card Tricks

A" and "B," and "Sawing a Woman in Half 107."
He wanted to postpone "Magic Potions 205" to
the fall term, but Gillian insisted on it from the
start for fear he'd never finish school. To spite
the Prince for this, Moondroth taught only the
most unimportant and evil-smelling potions — to
a point where the teacher himself had often to run
from the room holding his nose.

This course required mountains of memory
work. Each magic recipe called for innumerable
ingredients plus rituals and lengthy incantations,
all to be performed in precise sequence. For
instance, to improve the quality of goat's milk
— which didn't interest Gillian much anyway —
required thirty-four species of worms, twelve
toadstools, a marinade of beetle juice and varnish,
six stanzas from the national anthem, and finally
standing on one leg like a crane during the boiling.

Since much magic is done at night, school hours
were odd and irregular. Field trips were dependent
on the phase of the moon: some work requiring
the light and some the dark of it. A thunderstorm
was the signal to convene immediately. Damp and
dreary settings were invariably selected such as

bogs and leaky caves. Teacher, pupil and page all got runny noses, and there was a good deal of sneezing during the solemnities.

To make things worse, Moondroth mumbled so that Gillian couldn't catch half of what he said. Since the professor didn't like repeating himself, the result was that the Prince was forever getting his formulas wrong and having to do them over. Bats would come out of hats instead of rabbits. He would read his own mind instead of somebody else's. Mice stubbornly refused to turn themselves into horses or pumpkins into coaches. Professor Moondroth waxed crankier and crankier and mumbled all the more. He sent his pupil home with very bad report cards which plunged King Argoth into a fury.

The sleight-of-hand kind of magic came much easier to Quist than it did to Gillian, probably because he enjoyed it. He used to try it out on Thrag who was always astonished at finding a canary in the pocket of his leather apron or having an unexpected bug plucked from his ear. He would laugh delightedly at every new trick.

But one day Thrag grew solemn. He sat down

heavily on his anvil, shaking his head and staring at the floor.

"This kind of trick won't help Gillian at all," he said. "It's fun for you and it's fun for me, but it's only good enough for a court jester. It just won't do for a prince. Isn't he learning anything else?"

Quist told him about the magic potions meant to get rid of warts, prevent baldness or stop a toothache. Thrag's face darkened.

"None of those things are splashy enough. They're not like making the sun come out after a wet spell, even. Moondroth won't ever teach him a miracle. You know that, Quist, don't you? And King Argoth won't settle for anything less: nothing less than a worthwhile, community-service type of miracle."

Quist hadn't thought about that. He had been having a pretty good time in magic school and showing off his new tricks. Now he began to realize that he was right in the middle of another princely failure. Only this time was the most serious of all because the King had told Gillian this was his very last chance. It was knighthood or exile. Nothing in between.

He put the canary back in its cage and the bug in its box and left the smithy in silence.

Nor did he have a word to say to Gillian when, a little later, he climbed into his cot at the foot of the Prince's bed. He pretended to fall asleep immediately, even making convincing snoring noises, but actually he hardly slept that night at all. Bothersome thoughts buzzed around and around in his head.

Well before dawn, he slipped out of the tower room. Carrying his sandals, he ran barefoot down the circular stone stairs, raided the kitchen for a picnic lunch, and escaped to the harbor without anyone being the wiser.

There he took Gillian's boat and set sail for sea. As he thought of his troubles, he kicked the thwart of the little skiff and pointed her up into the wind. The early morning breeze began to freshen. Pretty soon there was a tug on the main sheet as the sail filled, and he became absorbed in the mere business of sailing. He felt the boat under him as it heeled and the water slapped at the bow.

The royal barge at anchor was soon passed and

quickly disappeared from view. The outer mole grew big as Quist approached it — then dwindled as he skimmed out into the open ocean. Ilfinore and Gillian and Argoth and the knights and ladies of the court and the pages and the grooms all blew out of his head like so many flimsy cobwebs.

He steered north with nothing, so far as he knew, between him and the top of the world.

But *that* was the morning that the sun came up just as the moon went down.

That was the morning, too, when Loquid set out on his wanderings.

And that was the morning they bumped into each other — and the noontime that Quist told the Sea Serpent all his troubles.

6

"Now that *is* quite a pickle," Loquid said as Quist finished his story. "Speaking of pickles, may I have another?"

Quist handed him one and the Sea Serpent rolled it around on his tongue, enjoying the bumps before swallowing it whole.

"Pickles help you think," he said.

Quist doubted it, but said nothing. He began worrying again (which is different from thinking). He had rather enjoyed the picnic and Loquid had been a good listener. But now he realized that not only had nothing been solved back in Ilfinore but that here he was stranded on a sandbar miles from home with a broken mast. He knew there was no way to mend it here. He would have no choice but to row home. Could he get back without anyone seeing him and put in a new mast? No. Not likely. Certainly not if he rowed straight into the busy harbor. His only hope was to put into a little uninhabited cove just west of the harbor, hide the boat overnight, and hope against hope that no one would notice it was missing from its mooring. It was a slim chance — really much too slim. He was mad at himself for only having made things worse for Gill and himself. Why had he hung about so long with this stupid Sea Serpent when every minute he was gone only made his absence more obvious?

He jumped up from the warm sandy spot he'd been sitting in, ran over to the boat, and began to furl the sail and stow the broken mast to make room for him to row. He set the oarlocks in their sockets and began pushing the boat toward the water.

All the while Loquid was eating and thinking. He lay still, idly watching Quist making preparations to leave. Then he began to smile. The smile broadened to a grin and the grin became a great GUFFAW!

"What's so *funny?*" Quist snapped. He was in no mood for jokes.

But once Loquid had begun to laugh, he couldn't stop. He chuckled and chortled helplessly and rolled over and over in the sand.

"Stop it!" Quist shouted. He thought Loquid

was laughing at him. "There's nothing funny in what I've told you, and nothing funny in what's coming next!"

"Oh yes there *is!*" said Loquid. And he burst out laughing again. "What comes next is *most* humorous," he chuckled. "Humorous and . . . and . . . and downright MAGNIFICENT! I told you that was a good omen this morning. Now just you listen to me."

Something in the Sea Serpent's tone got through to Quist. He stopped fussing around with the boat and paid attention.

Loquid had a plot. As he unfolded it, he got more and more excited until finally Quist caught his enthusiasm too. The page had to admit that it *was* magnificent. He began adding details of his own which the Sea Serpent delightedly accepted. When they had finished, they had worked up an admirable conspiracy.

"I guess we've got everything straight now," Loquid said. "You'd better get going."

"Right!" said Quist. He wanted to shake hands — but that is one thing clearly impossible with reptiles, seagoing or otherwise. He settled for an awkward wave before shoving off to sea.

The wind was at Quist's back, helping him, and he rowed as hard as he could, but it was still a long pull to Ilfinore. His back hurt and his hands were callused long before he got there.

This time he carefully skirted the mole, avoiding the harbor and making for the cove. Luckily he saw no other boats and was able to reach shore without being seen. The only mishap he had was in the cove itself when he was in such a rush to beach the boat that he fell overboard. He was dripping wet when he hauled it ashore and hid it in a little grove of alders.

Once sure the boat was well hidden, he turned and ran toward town. He was nimble-footed, and he was carried along by the excitement of his mission. He had never run faster in his life.

Where the sand turned to shingle at the town's edge, he stopped to put on his sandals — then ran on. An old man patching nets called out to him, but he didn't answer. Nor did he have a word for Thrag as he raced past his smithy. He avoided the town's main square, taking a side alley where he hoped to be less noticed, even though this route added a few precious minutes.

When he got to the castle gate, Grugeon was on duty. Quist groaned inwardly when he saw him. He tried to slip by, but the sentry barred his way with his lance.

"Where've *you* been, you young hellion?" Grugeon demanded.

"Nowhere! Let me by!"

"Nowhere indeed! I suppose a person goes nowhere in the Prince's boat."

Quist's heart sank. If Grugeon knew about the boat, then maybe everybody knew. But how much did he know?

"Smashed it up, I'll wager." He spat on the cobblestones. "Wrecked it. Stove a hole as big as a house. A wonder you didn't drown yourself — though it'd be a good thing if you had. Good riddance, I'd say. A lot of help *you've* been to Gillian!"

"We've been through all that," Quist snapped back. "Just let me by!"

"Don't you be shouting at me, you pointless

little page. You and your claims about Goroblast-catching! You and your stupid little parlor tricks! I'll not let you through this gate till you tell me the truth — and civil-like at that!"

It was very hard for the page to hold his temper and harder still to bear the delay, but he bit his lips and answered as civilly as he was able.

"I-have-not-wrecked-a-boat," he said, flatly.

"And who was asking you about *a* boat, you dunce," Grugeon said sarcastically, obviously enjoying himself. "I was asking about a very *specific* boat belonging to a certain well-known member of a certain royal family, name of Gillian. Now answer me straight, you useless piece of rubbish!"

He shook his lance for emphasis, glowering down at Quist from under his shaggy eyebrows.

"I-have-not-wrecked-Prince-Gillian's-boat."

"And how much truth is there in *that*, you little liar! Why would you be gone the whole day if you'd done no more than take a nice little sail, might I ask? And why would you be wet from head to foot, might I ask?"

Quist had to think fast. He had no answer for Grugeon's question, and even if he had, the guard could hold him up for an hour out of pure spite. He tried a desperate trick to distract his attention.

"Hey look, Grugeon!" he said in mock excitement. "There's Urga up there waving at you!"

"Where?" the guard asked, startled.

"Up there behind you where I'm pointing."

Grugeon turned to look and as he did so automatically raised his lance. That was all that Quist needed. He shot by him like an arrow and into the doorway of the cabbage room. In no time at all he had climbed the cabbage pile, wriggled through a small window and dropped into the narrow tunnel on the other side. He heard Grugeon's shouts behind him, but he knew he could neither follow nor find him now. Those weeks of exploring the castle paid off.

At the door to the tower he ran straight into Urga, blocking the entrance with her great bulk almost as effectively as Grugeon had barred the gate with his lance.

"Here, here! Where are you going in such a rush, small one?"

"Nowhere . . . to the Prince," Quist corrected himself. "He wants me right away."

76

"And I should think he might, little truant," Urga said. "Not seeing hide nor hair of you all day! But I'll not have you tracking dirt over my clean stairs, no matter how much of a rush you may be in. Off with your sandals!"

Angrily, Quist yanked them off and pushed by her. Halfway up the stair he couldn't resist calling back to her:

"Grugeon's looking for you. He's written another poem!"

From below he could hear the housekeeper utter a most unwomanly oath.

Gillian's greeting wasn't much better. The page's precipitate entrance had scared away a magpie on the window ledge that the Prince had been sketching.

"Now look what you've done!" Gillian complained in a rare fit of impatience. "Gone for the whole day, and now you've ruined my picture!"

"I know, Gill, but . . ."

"No buts now. I've spent the day covering up for you. I told them I'd *loaned* you my boat — otherwise you'd have been in a fine mess. All the guards would have been searching after you and

Grugeon the first of them all, I'll bet you."

Gillian tried scowling, drawing his eyebrows tight like his father. But it didn't suit him and he didn't scare Quist a bit.

"I'm already in a spot with Grugeon," Quist said. "But that's not important right now. What I want to tell you is . . ."

"Say, you look wet. You didn't capsize, did you?"

"No. I certainly didn't," Quist retorted with rising impatience.

"And I *do* hope you didn't smash up?"

"No! Gill, you've no more faith in me than anyone else!"

"Sorry," said Gillian. And he sounded it. His voice softened to its usual gentle tone. "It's not that I mind about your taking the skiff, but neither of us would hear the end of it if it's been smashed. If it's safe and sound again in the harbor we'll forget the whole thing."

Quist felt a momentary pang.

"The mast's broken and it's in the cove," he said, "but otherwise nothing's wrong. Besides, what I want to tell you is . . ."

"Oh *no*," Gillian groaned. "Oh Quist, how *could* you let it happen. It sounds like something *I'd* do — not you. Now we're in for it!"

"Now we aren't!" Quist interrupted. "And we've a good chance of getting out of trouble once and for all if you'll just *please* be quiet a minute and listen to me. We haven't got any *time!*"

"All right," Gillian sighed. He pushed back his easel and prepared to listen — though it was clear he didn't expect much of consequence.

But as Quist told him the plan, Gillian's eyes brightened. He began asking questions and taking a lively interest.

"It just might work," he said.

Together they got out a map of the town and planned what each would do.

"Should I be right here when it starts, do you think?" the Prince asked.

"It would seem most natural, wouldn't it? You usually *are* here this time of day."

Just then they heard the distant sound of shouting coming up from the town. But they could see nothing from the window except the last blinding rays of the sun as it sank into the ocean.

"That's the signal!" said Quist. "It's to start at sunset, and it's begun! I'll have to hurry."

And off he ran again, leaving Gillian staring out the window, squinting and trying as hard as he could to see what was out there.

The excited cries from the town had begun to echo in the castle courtyard by the time Quist got there. Grugeon was shouting at the top of his lungs, giving the alarm.

"To arms! To arms! The enemy cometh!" he bellowed — just as he had been taught to do on such an occasion. As he shouted, he pulled with all his weight on the bell rope at the gate, setting off a mighty clangor.

Out of the Great Hall and up from the jousting field poured the knights. The armorer stood in the armory door, swiftly handing out weapons. As each knight ran past, he grabbed a shield and a spear, hardly pausing in his dash.

Nobody knew what was happening, but rumors spread like weeds. One had it for certain that Lord Battledore was attacking. Another said it was more like Shuttlecock to break a treaty. That Shuttlecock was a sly one! Then it went around that the two lords had banded together and were surrounding the town. But when knights were dispatched to the hill behind the castle, they saw nothing more terrifying than a host of fireflies in the June night.

Reports from the harbor were less quieting. A fleet of a thousand ships was said to have been sighted off the mole. It must certainly be Lord Battledore — though even he hadn't a tenth that many ships in his fleet. It became definite that the two lords had banded together, having perfidiously laid their plans at the time of their state visit, and were now attacking Ilfinore without warning.

Quist slipped unnoticed through the gate this time. His affairs were no longer of interest to anyone. On all sides of him were knights in and out of armor, half visible in the swiftly darkening evening. In the town itself, the turmoil was even greater and rumors wilder. Women were swooning in the square from the sheer excitement of it all. Young girls were fanning them. Brave peasants were arming themselves with rakes and scythes against they knew not what. Cowardly ones were just as busy hiding.

Hordes of people were in motion — moving in

a great avalanche to the harbor's edge whence vast and hideous noises arose.

In and out of the crowd ran Quist, making his way across town to Moondroth's cliff. He found the magician sitting on a rock outside his door, his feet tucked up under him, swathed in his gray wool robe to keep out the evening damp, and staring wide-eyed at the scene below. Quist had never seen him look surprised before.

"Moondroth!" the page called breathlessly as he came up beside him. He tried to sound as though he was as terrified as the crowds he had just left. "Can't you *do* something? Can't you cast a spell?"

"I've no magic to fix *that*," Moondroth answered without once taking his eyes off the harbor. "Do you see what's going on?"

And so on Moondroth's hill, Quist got his first chance to have a look.

It was hard to make out just what was happening in the darkness, but the whole harbor was churning as though there were a hurricane tearing at the water. Yet the night was completely calm

without so much as a whisper of a wind. Mighty waves broke and crashed on the shingle. The boats at anchor broke their lines and popped into the air like so many drops of water on a hot skillet. The royal barge hove high on a great black hump — then plunged lumbrously on its side, and promptly sank. From beneath the waters came strange growling noises, first at one corner of the bay and then another. But the cause of all the disturbance was not, at that moment, visible.

The crowds of townsmen, peasants and knights ran about helplessly on the shore, waving their rakes and spears. Women and children higher up the slope behind them wept and wailed. Nobody seemed to have the least idea what was going on or what to do. Torches were ordered, illuminating the beach but casting no light on the mysterious goings-on.

Then a great shout went up, the crowds parted, and King Argoth appeared, mounted on his white stallion. Moondroth and Quist couldn't hear what he was saying from that distance, but he must have been giving orders because suddenly things happened. Trumpets blared. The knights formed themselves into tidy phalanxes. Archers appeared, knelt neatly on the beach and sent a flock of arrows soaring into the night. The crowd quieted so that one could hear the twang of the bows and the hiss of the arrows. But they had no effect on the raging sea, as one boat after another capsized with the unseen force.

Then out near the breakwater a spiraling fountain of flame burst from beneath the waters. A great "Ohhhhhhhh!" went up from the people of Ilfinore, like watchers at a fireworks display. The flame moved straight down the harbor, waxing bigger and brighter as it came and cutting through the turbulent waters like a knife. Men shook and women shrieked as it approached shore. The archers broke ranks, running from the waves that roared in on them. Even King Argoth, though sitting firm in his saddle, had to move back to keep from getting showered.

Up from among the breakers rose the gigantic head of a Sea Serpent, spouting fire and bellowing a great bellow. His whiskers stood out from his jaws like spikes. His eyes burned amber and changed to lustrous green. Then he reared and turned, thrashing his tail and plunging under the waters again.

More women fainted — and for better reason this time. The King's horse reared and nearly threw its rider. But even as Argoth clung to the stallion's neck, he issued further orders.

Up came the battering ram — but it had nothing to batter, going thump-thump into the empty air. It was followed by the giant sling which sent one rock after another into the water with no more effect than to sink another boat or two. The Sea Serpent continued his riotous writhings around the harbor, roaring and spitting flame.

"Moondroth! Moondroth!" came a shout from below. Page and magician turned to see a royal messenger struggling up the slope and waving.

"Come quick! The King needs you!"

Moondroth wrapped his cloak tighter around him. He did not budge.

"Quick!" the messenger repeated. "King Argoth needs your magic. You must save Ilfinore!"

"Ummmmmmmm . . ." the magician began, but had no more to say.

"Please hurry, Honorable Professor," the messenger pleaded. "We all need you."

He was shaking and looked very white in the face.

"I have no magic to halt a Sea Serpent," Moondroth mumbled, almost inaudibly.

This was the moment Quist had been waiting for.

"Prince Gillian has!" he broke in, stepping in front of the ancient man. "Tell the King to send for him!"

"He *what?*" the messenger asked, incredulous. "Don't joke with me *now.*"

"Prince Gillian knows how to stop him," Quist repeated.

"Is that *true?*" the messenger asked Moondroth.

"No doubt. No doubt quite true," Moondroth said. "You'd better go fetch him."

He retreated further into his cape as the messenger left reluctantly on his errand. Quist knew the magician didn't believe a word of it, but was only too glad to get out of a bad spot as he stalled for time.

"I never heard such a nonsensical idea," he muttered. "A fool like that who can't even get a card trick straight!"

Gillian was soon fetched, responding promptly for the first time in his life. Word spread before him that he would try magic. Scornful whisperings arose on all sides. "A waste of precious time," Urga muttered, and her neighbor nodded. Girls snickered and men fumed. Grugeon grunted and turned his back as the Prince passed him. Thrag looked uncomfortable as though he, too, was sure Gillian would make a fool of himself. King Argoth demanded silence and set his jaw as the Prince came up to him, giving no outward sign of his thoughts.

Gillian bowed solemnly to the King, and Argoth responded with a regal nod — an almost imperceptible inclination of his head. Then the Prince squared his shoulders and stalked with dramatic dignity to the top of the cliff where Quist awaited him. Torchbearers followed to make a circle of light. The populace below turned to watch, mumbling their doubts but oblivious for the moment of the great fiery thrashings in the harbor.

Quist put on a solemn look, too, as he stepped forward and made a show of fastening the gold buckle of the Prince's cape. Gillian mounted a boulder. He looked magnificent as he stood tall and trim in the torchlight, his legs astride and his cape floating out behind him. For a minute he stood perfectly still, staring gravely out to sea. Then he reached in his pocket and brought out his silver flute. After flourishing it three times in the air, he began to play a mysterious little tune, the notes slithering up and down the scale and the sound of it sending shivers up one's back.

A monstrous roar came from the harbor as Loquid's head and neck appeared again, silhouetted by his belching flames. But now the head began to sway in time with Gillian's pipings, back and forth and roundabout most gracefully. The thrashings ceased altogether and the waters became still. As the fires sank away, the crowd could just

make out a most beatific smile on the Sea Serpent's face.

Then Loquid turned and swam silently out of the harbor. The people gasped as they watched the last rippling coils disappear on the horizon.

Great shouts went up and cries of "Knight him! Knight him!" as the people turned again to look at Gillian. Thrag burst through the ring of torch-bearers and grabbed the Prince, hoisting him on his shoulders and carrying him to the King. Moon-droth, restored to his usual vigor, took Quist by the hand, fairly dragging him along behind him and whispering, "You had something to do with this, I'll wager!"

The crowd encircling the King gave way as magician and page appeared so that they both had a first-class view of the knighting. King Argoth dismounted for the ceremony, laying the flat of his sword on his son's shoulder and pronouncing him "Sir Gillian" in most ringing tones. Queen Argotha came flying up out of nowhere to enfold Quist in her diaphanous veils and give him a most embarrassing hug. She, like Moondroth, seemed convinced that the page was behind it all in some unfathomable way.

But neither Gillian nor Quist ever told the true story because both of them wanted it that way. Gillian was thereafter allowed to paint as much as he liked. His mural in the Great Hall became one of the wonders of Ilfinore, not to be missed by visitors and tourists, while the number of people in that land who took up art and music thereafter was astonishing. (More Muses had to be rushed in to take care of the demand.) Quist was presented with a boat of his own — which was what he wanted more than anything else in the world.

As for Loquid, he swam home that night to report most joyously that this had been the finest holiday of his life. Mrs. Loquid said "Hmmmmph!" But then, she always said something like that.